FLIKTOR

⌐HE DEADLY DESTROYER

With special thanks to Tabitha Jones

For Jennifer and Amy Reid

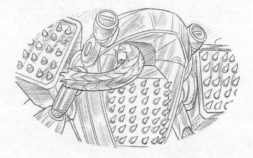

www.seaquestbooks.co.uk

ORCHARD BOOKS
Carmelite House
50 Victoria Embankment
London EC4Y 0DZ

A Paperback Original
First published in Great Britain in 2015

Series created by Beast Quest Limited, London

Text © Beast Quest Limited 2015
Cover and inside illustrations by Artful Doodlers,
with special thanks to Bob and Justin © Orchard Books 2015

ISBN 978 1 40833 480 5

1 3 5 7 9 10 8 6 4 2

Printed and bound by CPI Group (UK) Ltd, Croydon, CR0 4YY

MIX
Paper from
responsible sources
FSC® C104740

The paper and board used in this book are made from wood
from responsible sources.

Orchard Books is an imprint of Hachette Children's Group
and published by The Watts Publishing Group Limited,
an Hachette UK company.

www.hachette.co.uk

FLIKTOR
THE DEADLY DESTROYER

BY ADAM BLADE

ORCHARD

SIBORG'S HIVE LOG

DESTINATION: AQUORA

A plague is coming to Aquora!

Max and that pathetic Merryn girl
think they have defeated me, but
I have only become stronger. I
have analysed Max's weakness –
his love for his family! And soon
I will take from him all that he
holds dear.

I will do something my weak
father, the so-called Professor,
never could. Take over Aquora! And
I won't even need to fire a single
shot. The city will be mine, and
everyone in it my slaves!

Max couldn't have dreamt up the
horror I have in store for him,
even in his worst nightmares...

CHAPTER ONE

A NASTY BITE

"Hey, Lia! Take a look at this!" Max called into his headset, his finger hovering over the trigger for his aquafly's acid torpedoes. Through the domed glass cockpit of his new lightweight craft he could see Lia floating in the ocean nearby, twirling her new Merryn spear in one hand.

Beyond her, Max's dogbot Rivet and Lia's pet swordfish Spike were swooping through the sea-grass that surrounded Aquora. Lia lifted her hand, and threw a ball of seaweed out onto the current. Spike and Rivet streaked towards it. Rivet got there first, snapping up the seaweed in his metal jaws and veering away as Spike swerved after him.

Lia waved her hand through the water, washing off flakes of seaweed from her fingers, then spun to face Max, sighing theatrically. "What now?" she asked. "You know, I can only pretend to be interested in triple-luminosity headlights for so long."

Max grinned. "If that was you pretending to be interested, I'd hate to see you acting bored. Now watch this!" Max peered at his target, a rock with a cyrate's face projected onto it about fifty paces away, then pressed the red torpedo button.

Voom! The torpedo surged through the water and smashed against the rock, releasing a splat of sticky green acid. The acid bubbled and frothed, eating away at the rock behind the cyrate's face, then dripping down to leave a fizzing crater in the seabed.

"Wow. That's quite a mess you've made there," Lia said flatly.

"Exactly! Max said. "These torpedoes are designed to completely annihilate cyrates."

Lia shrugged. "I prefer good old Sumaran coral, personally," she said, jabbing her spear in a powerful thrust. "But I suppose metal-melting weapons could be useful, given your cousin's strange obsession with making evil robots. Although I was kind of hoping we'd seen the last of Siborg."

"Me too," Max said, "but something tells me that's unlikely." His stomach twisted with a familiar pang of dread at the thought of his evil cousin, but Max shrugged the feeling away and focussed back on his sleek new sub. "Anyway," he said, "if you think my torpedoes are cool, take a look at my jets!" Max flipped the cockpit open, swam out and ran his hand along the bullet-shaped thrusters. "With these I can go as fast over the surface of the water as I can beneath it, and if I power them up, I can even fly through the air! I reckon I could get as high up as my apartment. But you can't overload the thrusters for long or…" Max trailed off, noticing that Lia's gaze had drifted back towards Spike and Rivet.

"What's that thing Rivet's found?" Lia asked. Rivet was powering towards them, a blue oval object clasped between his teeth.

Rivet stopped at Max's feet, wagging his tail. Spike stayed a few paces away, eyeing the capsule nervously.

Max reached out a hand for the object and Rivet released it. It was as long as Max's forearm, and the surface was completely smooth and slightly warm to the touch.

"Rivet found lots!" Rivet barked, nodding

towards the sea-grass behind them.

"What is it?" Lia asked, leaning over to touch the object gently with a webbed finger.

"I've no idea," Max said, "but it doesn't look natural."

Suddenly Spike let out a flurry of warning clicks. Max turned and gasped. At least fifty more capsules had floated up from the sea-grass and were drifting towards them on the current. They were all the same size, and the same uniform blue. As one floated close to Spike, he jerked away, giving a high-pitched clack of alarm.

"Does Spike know what they are?" Max asked. Lia pressed her fingertips to her temples, using her Aqua Powers to communicate with her swordfish, then shook her head.

"He's never seen them before. But he doesn't like them one bit. And frankly, neither do I. They look far too much like tech to me."

"Hmmm," Max said, feeling a twinge of unease as he weighed the capsule in his hands. "I think I'll take this home and examine it in the lab."

"Good idea," Lia said. "I'll stay here with Spike." She glanced at her swordfish, who was watching wide-eyed as the tide of blue capsules flowed towards Aquora. "Those things have really got him spooked. I'll come and find you later."

"Good plan," Max said. He clambered back into his aquafly, tucked the capsule under the dashboard and patted the seat beside him. "Come on, Riv!" Max called to his dogbot. Rivet wagged his tail and jumped aboard.

Max closed the cockpit roof. As he threw Lia a wave through the window, he saw that there were more capsules than ever drifting around her. *What on Nemos are they?* he wondered, feeling another pang of anxiety. Then he gunned the aquafly's engines and veered towards Aquora. *There's only one way to find out.*

Max grinned as the rush of speed slammed him back in his seat, enjoying the ride despite his worries. His new design surged through the ocean, leaving barely a ripple in its wake.

It wasn't long before Aquora's skyscrapers cast long shadows over the water, blocking the sun from above. Max angled the aquafly upwards, breaking the surface beside the docks. He cut the engines, gliding neatly between two fibreglass jetties, then picked up the capsule and climbed ashore. Rivet jumped up beside him.

Ships and submersibles of every size crowded the docks. All around them, the water was thick with more blue capsules, bobbing between the vessels. Max frowned as he noticed a pile of them, washed up onto the man-made leisure beach further up the shore. People were bent over the pile, picking up the objects and holding them out for others to look at.

"Come on, Riv," Max said to his dogbot. "I'm getting a bad feeling about these things."

As Max headed inland towards his

apartment, the curved windows of Aquora's skyscrapers glittered in the morning sun. In the streets, huddles of people were inspecting capsules just like the one Max held.

People are bringing them into the city, thought Max, feeling uneasy.

When Max reached the entrance to his tower, Alpha 4, he swiped his key card and took the lift up to his apartment. Inside, he found his mother, Niobe, sitting at her desk looking down the eyepiece of her technoscope.

"Hi, Max's mum!" Rivet barked. Niobe pushed her red hair back from her face and looked up, smiling.

"Hi, Riv!" she said, then turned to Max. "How was your torpedo test-run?" she asked.

"Awesome," Max said. "But Mum, look!" He passed her the pale blue object. "Rivet found this in the sea-grass. Loads more have washed up all over Aquora. There must be thousands out there."

Niobe frowned, adjusting her technoscope to fit the capsule underneath. She squinted down at the shiny surface of the object.

"What do you think it is?" Max asked. Niobe looked up, her eyebrows knitting together in a puzzled frown.

"It's some sort of manmade polymer. But not one I've seen before." She held the oval up to her ear. "And there's something inside it," she said.

Max felt worry stirring in his stomach. *Could it be something to do with Siborg?*

Hwonk! Hwonk! Hwonk! Max and Niobe jumped as klaxons started howling outside, signalling that a city-wide emergency announcement was about to be made.

There was a crackle of static from the corner of the room, and the vidscreen flickered on. As Max glanced towards it, the bad feeling in his stomach got a thousand times worse. Gazing out of the screen, his pale, emotionless face half covered by a robotic mask, was Max's deadliest enemy – Siborg. Max gritted his teeth at the sight of his power-crazed, half-Merryn cousin. *I knew we hadn't seen the last of him.*

"Good morning, Aquorans," Max's cousin said, curling his lips into what could almost pass for a smile. "I'd like to introduce myself to you all. My name is Siborg, and I am an inventor. A visionary. You might almost call me your new master. In fact…" Siborg looked thoughtful for a moment then smiled. "Yes…I think I would like that. It will shortly be my very great pleasure to free you all from the wretched limitations of your puny human bodies and introduce you to the power of bio-robotics. And, as it would be quite useless to try and convince your inferior brains of the benefits of my technology, I have decided to *show* you instead. Behold the power of Siborg!"

The vidscreen went blank, and at the same moment a hideous, high-pitched screech blared through the loudspeakers outside. Max clapped his hands over his ears. Niobe did the same, and Max noticed the blue capsule on her desk had started to judder. Suddenly it cracked open, and Max watched in horror as hundreds of shiny, metallic-looking beetles swarmed out.

"Ahhh!" Niobe screamed as the beetles scuttled up her arms. Max lunged towards her as she tried to bat them away, but more insects were already flowing off the desk towards him. Rivet barked and leapt towards them, snapping his metal jaws, but the beetles swerved around the dogbot towards

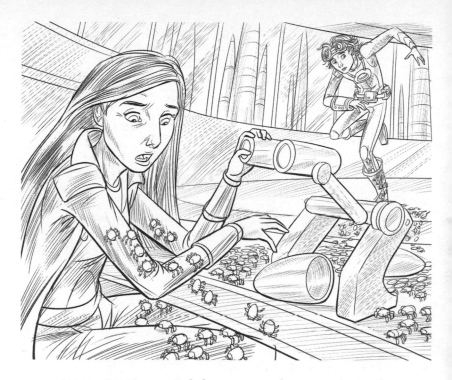

Max. He jumped from one foot to the other as they scurried up his legs and body, inside his clothes. Thousands of tiny pattering feet prickled his skin.

There was a sharp pain at the base of his skull, then a rush of warmth. The ground beneath him seemed to tip. His legs buckled, and the last thing he heard before he sank into darkness was Rivet's frantic barking.

#
OVERRUN

Max felt a cool pressure on his face, pulling him out of the darkness. It took a moment to work out what it was – Rivet's metal tongue. Max opened his eyes to find himself looking straight up his dogbot's nose. Rivet stepped back, panting anxiously.

"Okay, Max?" Rivet asked. Max sat up slowly, frowning as he tried to focus his bleary eyes. His tongue felt thick and dry and his brain was foggy. He glanced around the room, trying to remember what had happened. Then his guts clenched as he saw his mother slumped across her desk, with the remains of the broken capsule beside her.

"Mum!" Max cried, but she didn't stir. He shook himself and jumped up, remembering the prickle of tiny feet all over his body. The creatures were gone, but he could still feel a nagging pain at the back of his neck. Max lifted his hand and felt something the size of his thumb attached to his skin. He dashed it off, shuddering with horror as a shiny blue beetle landed on the floor with a metallic ping. He stamped on it hard, cracking it open to reveal a mass of tiny wires and chips.

"Mum!" Max called again, rushing to her side. She had a beetle fastened to the base of her skull too. Max grabbed it and yanked it off, and immediately Niobe began to stir. She sat up slowly, holding a hand to her head.

"What happened?" she asked.

Max pointed at the blue beetle lying belly-up on the desk. "A whole swarm of those robot bugs hatched from that egg," Max said. "They bit our necks and knocked us out."

"Siborg," Niobe said, grimacing.

Max nodded.

"I'll call your father," Niobe said, tapping her communicator and putting it to her ear. Max waited, but Niobe shook her head. "No answer," she said. Her expression was grave.

"Switch on the vidscreen," Max told Rivet. "If that screech opened all the capsules, it should have made the news."

Rivet turned towards the vidscreen and it flickered on, but showed only static. Rivet's eyes flashed as he changed channels.

It was the same on every one. Max could feel his chest getting tight and his heart racing. He ran to the window, but the ground was too far below to see any detail.

"If all those capsules opened…" he said. Then a jolt of fear stabbed through him. "I left Spike and Lia surrounded by them!"

Niobe frowned. "Let's take a look outside and find out what's going on."

They headed out of the apartment and took the elevator downwards.

When they reached the sunny street, Max

gasped. It was silent. The hovercars had stopped, their passengers slumped in their seats. The pavements were strewn with people lying where they had fallen. Max could see the glint of metal bugs on the backs of their necks. He dropped to the side of a woman nearby whose chest was rising and falling steadily.

"Let's get the bugs off them," Max said.

"Maybe they'll wake up."

"Good plan," Niobe said, crossing to a suited man. Max curled his fingers around the bug attached to the woman at his side, but her arm suddenly jerked upwards, grabbing hold of his wrist.

"Ow!" Max cried. He tried to pull his arm away as the woman sat up, but her grip was like a vice. Then she turned towards him, and Max felt an icy chill. Her eyes were blank and staring, the pupils tiny fixed points. Niobe rushed to Max's side and grabbed the woman's shoulder while Max twisted his arm free. The woman struggled and writhed, but together, Max and Niobe held her down on the pavement, kneeling either side of her.

"Mum! Look!" Max said, nodding towards the beetle on the woman's neck. A red light on its head was blinking on and off. "It must be controlling her," Max said, shuddering with horror. "Rivet! Go and warn Lia to get as far away from those capsules as possible!"

"Yes, Max!" Rivet barked, bounding away.

"We should get this woman to the infirmary," Niobe said.

"But how?" Max said, gritting his teeth with the effort of holding the woman still. "She won't stop fighting us!" Max glanced up to see the suited man nearby starting to rise clumsily to his feet. But then his blank eyes fixed on Max and Niobe and he lurched towards them. Max gasped as he saw that all the people in the street were doing the same.

"Mum, I think it's time to get out of here!" Max said. "Run!"

Max and Niobe sprang to their feet.

"That way!" Max shouted, pointing to a gap in the approaching mob. He raced forwards, dodging the grabbing fingers of wide-eyed old ladies and teenagers. He recognised the round-faced baker from his favourite cake shop, and bundled past, knocking the heavy man aside.

"Yah!" Niobe shouted, kicking a black-clad teen out of their way.

They hurtled onwards towards the street corner. Max could feel his breath rasping in his chest and adrenaline pumping through him. Around the corner, he stopped dead. Beside him, his mother groaned with dismay. There were at least thirty people stumbling towards them, their eyes as blank as dolls'.

Max barrelled his shoulder into the door of a shop. It flew open and he tumbled inside. Niobe darted in after him, slamming the door and throwing her weight against it. Max grabbed a shelving unit and shoved it against the door as fists started to hammer on the outside. Then he and his mother raced into a rear stockroom. Max slammed and locked the door, then leaned against it beside his mother. They looked at each other, panting, as the banging got louder.

"I'm starting to wish I'd stayed in bed today," Niobe said. "What's going on?"

"It's like they're all possessed!" Max said. "Siborg's done something awful to them

with those bugs."

"But why aren't we affected?" Niobe asked, grimacing at the sound of breaking glass. "And how on Nemos can we get out of here?"

Then the thudding started. Max could feel the door at his back juddering as it was hammered by fists. The hinges cracked and the wood splintered.

"This door isn't going to hold," Max said, glancing around the storeroom. There was no way out. "What now?"

"I'm guessing negotiation is out of the question," Niobe said.

Then Max heard a familiar voice shout out behind the door: "Everybody stand back!" Relief flooded through him.

"Dad!" Max cried. The banging stopped, and Max heard the footsteps backing away.

"Thank goodness!" Niobe said, flicking the lock on the door and pushing it open.

Outside, Max could see his father dressed in military black, a horde of glassy-eyed Aquorans pressed up behind him. Max stepped forwards, but something about the look on his father's face made him stop dead.

"You are under arrest," Callum said, his empty eyes flicking from Max's face to Niobe's. "Seize them!" he ordered, gesturing to the mob behind him. Two burly Aquoran Defence Officers stepped towards Niobe.

"Callum!" Niobe cried desperately as the guards grabbed her. Max backed away, but before he could reach the door, two more guards lunged and gripped his shoulders so hard it hurt. Callum turned and strode away, the Aquorans around him parting to make way. Max saw a small blue beetle clinging to the base of his father's skull, and his stomach churned with dread.

Not Dad too!

CHAPTER THREE

MINDBUGS

As Max and Niobe were pulled along behind Callum, Max could hear the shuffling footsteps of the crowd from behind.

"Dad!" Max called. "It's me, Max! You have to listen!" But Callum marched on.

"Callum!" Niobe cried. "This isn't you. You need to fight that thing on your neck!" Callum's step didn't even falter. A chill crept over Max's skin, despite the warm sun. *What if Dad stays like this for ever?*

At last they reached the high, glass-walled

skyscraper that housed the Aquoran Council Chambers. The doors swung open, and Callum beckoned for Max and Niobe to follow him inside, leaving the silent crowd in the street.

He led them through the sleek entrance hall and into a bullet-shaped lift. The doors slid shut, and Max felt his stomach lurch as the lift shot upwards.

"Please, Dad," he tried one more time, but Callum just ignored him.

When the lift jerked to a stop, a bland female voice echoed from the speakers above. "Council Chambers."

Callum strode out, straight through the carpeted lobby and into the council chamber beyond.

Max and his mother exchanged a worried glance, then followed.

The Council Chamber was a huge circular

room, walled from floor to ceiling with smoked glass. The docks were visible far below, and beyond that, the sparkling ocean. Around the room, the council members were seated, staring with dull, glazed eyes towards a raised chair at the back – the seat of Chief Councillor Glenon. Max followed their gaze, and his stomach jolted with horror.

Sprawled across the chair, with Callum at his side, sat Siborg. He was gazing back at Max and Niobe with a bored expression on his half-metal face. Anger flared in Max's chest.

"What have you done to my dad?" he demanded.

"Greetings," Siborg drawled, ignoring Max's outburst. "So, my mindbugs didn't work on you then?" He tapped his teeth thoughtfully. "Irritating. But not outside the scope of my calculations. I thought

those with the Merryn Touch might prove troublesome. Which is why I had you all brought here."

Siborg lifted a hand and waved towards a side chamber.

Max felt a flicker of hope. *Is there someone else in Aquora with the Merryn Touch who might be able to help?* But his hope was quickly smothered as the Professor stepped through the doorway with an Aquoran guard on each side. *Siborg must have released his father from prison so they could work together*, Max thought.

One of the Professor's guards was none other than Lieutenant Jared – the self-serving coward who had almost got Max killed. Not only that, Jared had almost allowed Aquora to be destroyed by the colossal Robobeast, Drakkos. *Great*, Max thought. *All my favourite people working together.*

"Son!" the Professor called, smiling as Siborg turned towards him. "I knew only you could conquer Aquora! With your intelligence and knowledge of tech, you truly are a chip off the old block."

Siborg turned his gaze on his father, and his eyes blazed with anger. He reached for a control pad on the arm of his chair. Suddenly the Professor grimaced as his arms slammed together before him. Magnetic manacles were attached to his wrists, and they were now held tightly together.

Siborg must have activated them! Max realised.

Siborg turned away from his father and back to Max. "Now that we've got that embarrassing outburst out of the way," he said, "it's time to choose my guinea pig. I need to hone my mindbugs to control those with the Merryn Touch, but I really only need one subject." Siborg narrowed his eyes at Max and Niobe, and then at the Professor. "Ip, dip, sky blue," he said, pointing at each of them in turn. Then he grinned. "I choose… you." His finger pointed at Niobe. "I'll enjoy executing the other two far more. And it will be nice to have a fully functioning set of parents after mine turned out to be so staggeringly useless. Won't it, Dad?"

Max glanced at the Professor in confusion. But the answer came from his own father, at Siborg's side.

"Indeed it will, son," Callum said, flashing Siborg a blank-eyed smile. "I really am the luckiest father alive to have a son like you." Niobe gasped, and Max felt sick with fury.

"Simon!" the Professor hissed sharply. "You've spent too long alone with your gadgets and toys. You've gone completely insane!"

Siborg raised an eyebrow. "I wonder who I could have got that from?" he said. Then his face twisted with hatred and spite as he jabbed a button on the pad by his hand. The cuffs around his father's wrists crackled and sparked with electricity, and the Professor yelped with pain. Siborg grinned. "That should help you remember," he said. "My name is Siborg now."

Max caught a movement from the corner of his eye. He glanced towards it, and grabbed his mother's arm, hope surging through him. Outside, his aquafly was swooping towards the glass wall of the chamber, thrusters firing at full throttle. Max could just make out Lia at the controls with her Amphibio mask covering her face, and Rivet at her side. As Max watched, a torpedo shot from the sub. *Go Lia!*

Splat! The torpedo hit the chamber wall, spattering green acid across the glass.

Siborg turned and glanced at the sticky mess with a look of distaste. Then his expression turned to alarm as the window bubbled and started to dissolve.

"Let's go!" Max yelled. Niobe nodded, and together they sprinted across the room. Lia flipped the lid of the aquafly as they pounded towards her.

"Stop them!" Siborg shouted. As Max and Niobe streaked past, Jared and the Professor's other guard lunged towards them. Max lifted his elbow and jabbed Jared hard in the ribs, throwing him back. Niobe spun and sent the second guard flying with a roundhouse kick to the chest, then raced onwards towards the gap in the glass wall. As Max got close, his stomach clenched at the sight of the docks spread far below him. *If we fall…*

He held his breath and leapt. His legs windmilled in the air as Siborg screamed with rage.

Thump! Max landed in the aquafly.

Thud! Niobe came down beside him. The tiny craft tipped and swayed as they scrambled into the cramped cockpit seats.

Max could hear the engines straining as the overcharged jets struggled with the extra weight.

"Maybe I could get used to this technology stuff after all," said Lia, grinning.

"Rescue Max!" Rivet barked, wagging his tail by the pilot's seat.

"You guys are awesome!" Max said. "But now we'd better get out of here!" He shut the cockpit roof and grabbed the control stick, but before he could steer, a shadow blocked the sun from above. Max looked up to see the Professor falling towards them, his arms still clamped together and his legs pedalling in the air.

"Oof!" The Professor landed across the windshield like a splatted fly. The thruster jets made a terrible stuttering sound as the aquafly tipped onto its side, then plummeted.

Max gasped as he was thrown against Lia, while Niobe was crushed against him from the other side. The Professor had somehow looped his manacled hands around the aquafly's lower fin, and was being tugged downwards by the craft, his tunic billowing against the windscreen and his feet pointed towards the sky. Below, Max could see the glittering docks of Aquora racing towards them at sickening speed.

"Falling, Max!" Rivet barked.

Thanks, Rivet.

Max could hardly move, sandwiched between Lia and his mum. But he had to do something.

He reached a hand toward the controls, grabbed the control stick and tugged. The engines screamed. *There isn't enough power!* He stretched out his fingers, holding his breath with the effort as he just managed to flick the emergency bypass switch.

There was a hum as the backup batteries powered up. *Yes!* It would only give him seconds of thrust, but with luck that should be enough to land. Max tugged the controls, his body jolting upright as the aquafly righted and the thrusters engaged. Lia cried out as she was jerked about in her seat. Niobe was holding onto the control panel, her face completely grey.

As they swooped towards the docks, Max held the craft steady, lining them up with a fibreglass jetty. *We're losing height way too fast*, he realised, tensing his muscles against the impact.

Smash! Max's bones jolted. Lia and Niobe cried out in pain. The aquafly skidded forward. It bounced, once, twice…then came to a stop almost at the end of the jetty.

Niobe and Lia sat, frozen. Then Niobe let

out a shaky breath.

"I never did like flying," she said.

"Are you okay?" Max asked Lia.

She nodded slowly, her eyes still wide with terror. "I take back what I said about technology though."

Rivet scrambled out from under Max's seat and wagged his tail.

"Fun ride, Max!" he said.

Max flipped the lid of the aquafly and clambered onto the jetty. Along the length of the fibreglass walkway, the sea slapped and foamed. Max felt his anger flare as he saw the Professor sitting beside the craft, holding his head and blinking.

The Professor looked up, and smiled. "Well, that blew away the cobwebs!" he said. "Although I have to say, I would have preferred a smoother landing."

Max gritted his teeth in fury. "You almost

killed us all!" he said. "What were you thinking?"

"The same as you," the Professor said. "I was trying to escape from my lunatic son. Which, I feel I must point out, we don't seem to have achieved."

The Professor pointed towards the sea road that ran along the shore. It was as crowded as if it were a public holiday. But the people there weren't eating ice cream. They were marching steadily towards the docks, their blank eyes glinting in the sun.

CHAPTER FOUR

A TERRIBLE SACRIFICE

"We have to get out of here!" Lia cried.

"We can't," Max said. "The aquafly's fuel cells are dead." He saw military aircraft taking off from the roof of the council chamber, speeding towards the docks. "They won't take long to recharge, but longer than we've got, by the look of it."

"Then we'll just have to make some time," Niobe said, leaping from the aquafly.

Lia jumped down beside her, smiling grimly

as she twirled her spear around and pointed the butt towards the approaching crowd. The first aircraft had reached the quay and was coming in to land. People flowed out of its path without even looking up, as if they were being controlled like puppets, by a single master. *Which of course they are…* Max thought bitterly.

"Ahem!" The Professor lifted his manacled hands towards Max. "I won't be much help like this," he said. "Why not unlock these and pass me a weapon?"

"Maybe because you're a crazy super-villain?" Max said. He lifted his hyperblade and turned towards the crowd. The first of the officers from the aircraft reached the end

of the jetty. It was Lieutenant Jared. *Just what I need!* A group of mindless-looking civilians were marching behind the lieutenant. "If you want to help," Max told the Professor, "keep an eye on the aquafly's recharging fuel gauge. Tell us when she's ready. But don't even think about taking off. I have a remote control." The Professor glanced at Jared, and a look of alarm flickered across his face.

"An excellent idea!" he said, then he turned and scrambled into the armoured aquafly.

Niobe, Lia and Rivet stood at Max's side, ready for the attack. Jared lunged straight for Max, waving a blaster. "I'm taking you in!" he said, his thin lips twisted into an ugly smile. Max assumed he was being controlled by a mindbug, but it was hard to tell with Jared.

"Sorry, Lieutenant," Max said, lifting his hyperblade and wincing as he brought the hilt down on Jared's head. The man dropped like a stone, and Max felt a flicker of guilty satisfaction thinking of the headache the conniving officer would have when he awoke.

Lia and Niobe were swinging their weapons in wide arcs, keeping the rest of the crowd back while Rivet growled and barked.

"Half full!" the Professor called.

Max bit his lip, frustration and anxiety building inside. More aircraft were landing on the quay, and Max could see military ships gliding away from a jetty further along the shore. *We're going to be surrounded!*

"Max," Niobe said, grunting as she jabbed a citizen away, "the aquafly can't carry us all. And unfortunately the Professor's the only person in Aquora with the know-how to destroy those mindbugs. You and Lia have to take him to Siborg's ship. It's our only hope."

Max couldn't fault her argument. "But what about you?" he said, dreading the reply.

"I'm going back to the Council Chambers. If Siborg wants me to be his mum –" Niobe cringed at the word – "he's not likely to kill me."

Max swung his blade threateningly at a burly dockhand, who dodged back out of reach. "Siborg said he wouldn't kill you, but he also said something about experiments."

"So you'll have to work out how to stop him quickly," Niobe said. Their eyes met briefly. "I trust you, Max," said his mum. Raising her hands, she walked towards the crowd.

"Full!" the Professor called over to them.

"Go!" Niobe shouted over her shoulder, as the dockhand and a gangly teenager grabbed her by the arms and dragged her away. The rest of the crowd surged forward, waving sticks and other makeshift weapons.

Max felt sick, but he had no choice. The only way to save his parents now was to defeat Siborg. He turned and raced to the aquafly, then jumped aboard. Lia scrambled into the seat beside him and Rivet landed on his lap. As Max closed the cockpit roof, fists and weapons pounded hard on the toughened glass. Max gunned the engines and the aquafly surged into the sea with an almighty splash.

Underwater, everything was calm and quiet. Lia greeted Spike with a wave as he

came alongside the aquafly. There were still a few blue capsules floating towards the city, and the sight of them gave Max an idea. He turned the aquafly against the current.

"Good plan," the Professor said approvingly. "The capsules arrived on the current, so if you follow it out to sea, you'll reach their source."

Max grunted. He might be stuck with the Professor, but he wouldn't make small talk.

"You know, I'm quite impressed Simon managed to get those bugs to work," the Professor said. "He's a bright lad, but still, the technology involved is astounding."

Max rounded on the Professor, so angry his pulse thumped in his ears. "Look," Max said, "that technology just happens to be controlling my father, and your son is going to be doing experiments on my mother, so if you don't mind keeping your mouth shut –"

"Max," Lia said, touching his shoulder, "I

don't trust him either, but as your mum said, he does know tech. He might be able to help."

"Exactly," the Professor said, grinning. "In fact, I suspect I know a whole lot more than my evil genius wannabe son."

Yeah, right, Max thought. He gritted his teeth and stared ahead. He didn't like it, but Lia had a point. "Okay," Max said grudgingly. "What do you know about mindbugs?"

"Well," the Professor said, rubbing his jaw, "I almost mastered the technology once, before I got distracted by other projects."

"You mean you couldn't get them to work," Max said.

"If you must put it like that, yes," the Professor said. "In any case, I'm sure if you got hold of one, I could tell you how to destroy it. But first…" He squirmed in his seat, his shoulders cracking. "Take these manacles off me. I'm not going to help anyone while I'm trussed up like a common prisoner."

Max gritted his teeth. "Fine," he said at last. "Rivet, deactivate the cuffs."

"Sure, Max?" Rivet asked.

"Not really, Riv," Max said, "But Lia's right. We don't have a choice."

Rivet touched the tip of his nose to the Professor's cuffs, and there was a hum as his electromagnets engaged. The cuffs opened, and the Professor's hands sprang apart.

"Much better," he said. "You know, Max, you really are a lot more agreeable than my son. Which gets me thinking. If I assist you in defeating his plans, maybe Aquora would consider pardoning me –"

"Let's not get ahead of ourselves," Max said. "And anyway, what is it between you and Siborg? He seemed ready to have you killed back at the Council Chambers."

"An all too common story, I'm afraid," the

Professor said. "I was tied up in my work when he was small. If I'd known he had an aptitude for the family business, I would have got him involved, but…" He shrugged elaborately. "It's rather too late now, don't you think?"

"So you abandoned your own son?" Lia said. "Nice. No wonder he's so well adjusted."

A soft beeping from the dashboard cut into the conversation. A glowing shape had appeared on the aquafly's scanner – a huge, spherical vessel that Max recognised only too well. Siborg's ship. The *Hive*.

"Lia," Max said. "Tell Spike to lie low. I'm going to take the aquafly up to the surface – Siborg will be expecting us to attack from underwater, so let's give him a surprise."

Lia nodded and put her fingers to her head for a moment, using her Aqua Powers. Max saw Spike flick his tail, and dive deeper into the shadowy blue below.

Max climbed through the water, glancing about for cyrates. There were craggy towers of grey rock, and in the distance an underwater mountain, but Max couldn't see anything moving at all. The water grew brighter and clearer as they neared the surface. Just before they broke through the waves, Max hit the thrusters, setting the aquafly to glide mode.

They pushed out of the sea into a wide arch of clear blue sky spread over rolling waves and jutting rocks. Dead ahead, Max could see the dark form of the *Hive*, bloated and ugly with guns poking from its metal sides.

"Not a bad effort," the Professor said, running his eyes over his son's ship as they skimmed over the waves towards it.

"Glad you're enjoying yourself," Max said, frowning at the arsenal before him. "But if you have any idea how to get inside – Whoa! What is that?" A glittering silver coil lashed

across the surface of the water towards them.

Before anyone could answer, the end of the coil slapped against the aquafly's window and wrapped around its wing. The aquafly lurched and Max struggled to keep it steady. Lia and the Professor were thrown against each other, and Rivet flew from Max's lap as the aquafly was pulled roughly from the sunlit surface, back below the water…

CHAPTER FIVE

FLIKTOR ATTACKS

Max peered through swirling bubbles to see the hulking silver form of a Robobeast kicking towards them. He could barely believe his eyes – it was a giant frog. Its long metal tongue was wrapped around the craft like a lasso, and on either side of the frog's ram-like head, Max could see a colossal rocket launcher teeming with spiked torpedoes. The frog's robotic body was armoured like a tank, and it had dazzling

LED eyes, each as big as the aquafly. Etched onto the robot's silver belly Max could see a single word: *Fliktor*.

"Magnificent," the Professor muttered, still crushed against Lia, staring out at the gigantic robot with an expression of horrified awe.

The frog suddenly dived, and Max felt a jolt as the aquafly tipped and plunged, snatched

downwards by the Robobeast's tongue. Max's stomach lurched. Clouds of silt churned all about them. It was hard to tell up from down. Max pulled on the controls and hit the thrusters, but the engines whined. The robot's tongue was too strong.

"Max!" Lia cried. "We're going to crash!" The rocky seabed was looming towards them, dark and craggy, and the craft wasn't slowing at all.

"Not if I can help it," Max said. "I'm cutting us free." He hit the emergency escape and shot out into the water through a chute in the floor of the craft. Fliktor's bright eyes cast beams towards him like giant torches, and its rocket-launchers gleamed.

Max powered along next to the sinking aquafly, pulling his hyperblade from his belt. He grabbed hold of Fliktor's tongue and started hacking. The tongue was made of narrow links, like the vertebrae of a snake. Max felt a wave of panic building inside him as he cut. The metal was super-strong, and the seabed was getting closer and closer. He didn't have time! But then Max heard a flurry of clicks, and a moment later Spike was at his side, slicing at the tongue with his sword.

One after another, Max's hyperblade and Spike's sword bit into the metal again and again. Finally… *Yes!* Fliktor's severed tongue snapped back towards the frog's wide mouth, like an elastic band. The section wrapped about the aquafly uncoiled and the aquafly swooped upwards with Lia at the controls.

They made it! Then Max glanced towards the robot frog, and terror seared through him. The Robobeast's mouth was open, and deep within its bulging throat, Max could see even more rows of torpedoes.

The Robobeast's LED eyes turned red.

"Spike! Go!" Max shouted. Spike flicked his tail and dived behind a rock jutting from the seabed, just as a tremendous explosion rang out around them.

BANG! Fliktor recoiled like a giant cannon and a flash of light left Max blinded. He blinked, and when his vision cleared he saw a swarm of red-tipped torpedoes zooming towards the aquafly.

His heart thundered as he darted towards his craft ahead of the missiles. Lia's eyes were wide as she stared through the watershield. Max climbed onto the roof of the craft and hammered on the glass, pointing frantically at the trigger for the aquafly's acid torpedoes. Lia jerked into action, fumbling with the controls and hitting the lights by mistake. Max glanced at the rockets powering toward him and froze, paralysed by fear. *We're going to be blown to pieces!*

But then the Professor shouldered Lia aside, grabbed the controls, aimed and hit *fire*. Two acid torpedoes shot from the aquafly towards the approaching missiles. The torpedoes collided and green acid exploded out into the water. A group of Fliktor's missiles foamed and fizzled away. But more than half were left, and they were so close Max could feel their current. Max clung to the roof of the aquafly, holding his breath, his whole body tensed with terror.

Suddenly, the aquafly beneath him surged upwards. Max's stomach flipped. Water rushed past him, buffeting him, flattening him to the roof of the craft. He couldn't move. He could hardly breathe. Though the glass roof of the aquafly he could see the Professor at the controls, firing the thrusters at full throttle. The pressure on Max's body was so great that the edges of his vision started to fade. *Is he trying to kill me?* The water around Max got suddenly brighter, then droplets burst around him in a glittering spray as the aquafly shot into the air.

Boom! There was a huge explosion below as the torpedoes hit the surface of the ocean. Max felt the aquafly surge upwards, a fountain of water flinging it into the sky. It tipped and started to spin. Max couldn't keep his grip. His fingers slipped and his body tumbled through the air like a ragdoll.

Splash! Max plunged back into the sea. As soon as he was under, he could see the wide beams cast by Fliktor's massive eyes. The Robobeast's broad, armoured head was cannoning towards him as its vast feet ploughed through the water.

Time for a battle! Max thought, drawing his hyperblade. But as he swung it towards the approaching Robobeast, his stomach clenched with fear. He didn't know how long he could last against the giant robot alone. *Was this the Professor's plan all along?*

Max met the Robobeast head on. Fliktor's mouth opened and his snake-like tongue flicked out. Max was ready for it and kicked upwards out of reach, darting forwards to land on top of the robot's head. Max scrambled down onto Fliktor's neck, looking for a control box. But there was nothing. Just thick armour. Spike swam towards Max and started to jab at the robot's back with his sword, but he didn't even leave a dent.

Suddenly the Robobeast kicked out its massive back legs and surged forwards. Max flew off Fliktor's back, spinning head over heels. When he managed to right himself, he found Fliktor had turned, and was staring back towards him, mouth gaping wide and spiked torpedoes glistening. Max swam as fast as he could, but when he glanced back over his shoulder, the Robobeast was right behind him. Fliktor's rocket launchers were aimed at him at point-blank range.

Max's body tensed in horror as Fliktor's eyes turned red. *This is it!* Then something grabbed the back of his suit and pulled. Max looked up to see the Professor leaning from the aquafly above him. Max grabbed the

Professor's free hand and scrambled into the craft next to Lia, who was clinging on for dear life. The Professor closed the cockpit and gunned the engines, surging away from Fliktor's bristling torpedoes.

"Sorry about the bumpy ride," the Professor said. "I had to take some evasive action." He gestured for Max to take the controls, as Rivet leapt into Max's lap.

Max's blood was still thundering through his veins. He could hardly believe he was alive. But there was still a robotic rocket launcher just behind them.

He took a deep breath and hit the thrusters, sending the aquafly steeply upwards. They soared out of the ocean, into bright daylight. The dark, orb-shaped *Hive* was dead ahead. Max put his foot down hard, boosting the aquafly's thrusters and pushing them up into the sky. When Max was sure they were out of reach of Fliktor's tongue, he finally levelled the craft, aiming straight for Siborg's ship.

"FOREIGN CRAFT APPROACHING TO THE REAR," the aquafly's speakers blurted. Max glanced back to see Fliktor leap off an island of rock and soar upwards over their craft, plunging them into shadow. Max gritted his teeth. *Of course! Frogs don't just swim. They jump.*

CHAPTER SIX

HIVE WITHIN A HIVE

The frog's tank-like body plunged towards them.

SMASH! The force of its impact on the aquafly jarred Max's spine and threw him forwards. Lia grabbed the dashboard as the vessel plummeted back into the ocean. Spike surged up to meet them as Max scrabbled with his controls, steadying the aquafly underwater and keeping them angled towards the *Hive*.

"TURN BACK NOW OR YOU WILL BE DESTROYED," a cold robotic voice blurted through the aquafly's communication speakers.

"Cyrates!" Lia cried, pointing ahead. The skeletal, black forms of Siborg's evil creations were pouring from the bottom of the *Hive* into the water, red eyes blazing. They zoomed towards the aquafly, faster than Max had ever seen a cyrate move. As they sped closer, Max could see why. These cyrates didn't have feet, or even flippers. Instead, they had powerful thrusters attached to their legs.

Max grabbed a blaster from under the dashboard and handed it to Lia.

"What do I do with this?" Lia asked.

"Point it at the baddies and fire!" Max said.

Lia scowled and grabbed her spear, but Max was glad to see that she kept hold of the blaster too. He took another for himself, then drew his hyperblade.

"I can't believe I'm doing this," he said, holding the hyperblade out to the Professor. "But take this. And make sure you get to the *Hive*. We're going to need your evil genius to defeat your son."

"How kind," the Professor said. "I will do my best not to die." Max jammed the aquafly's steering column to keep it zooming through the water, then hit the release for the roof.

"Everyone out!" Max cried. Max, Lia, Rivet and the Professor all leapt from the aquafly, just as Fliktor's tongue came rushing from behind, wrapped around the aquafly and snatched it away. *I just hope chewing on the craft keeps Fliktor busy long enough for us to reach the* Hive, Max thought.

The next moment the cyrates were on them. Lia leapt onto Spike's back and surged ahead, spear raised and blaster blazing.

Max dived alongside her and started
firing. Red energy bolts zoomed through
the water and exploded against the cyrates,
blasting their bodies apart. Fragments of
black metal floated down, but more cyrates
zoomed through the debris, red eyes glowing
and guns blazing. As Lia and Spike dodged

between flashing energy bolts, Lia swung her spear, smashing off robotic arms and legs. Rivet growled and snapped at the robots as he whizzed towards the *Hive*. The Professor slashed with Max's hyperblade. Luckily, like Max, he had the Merryn Touch, and was just as at home underwater as Max and Lia.

Max fired his blaster again and again, aiming at pairs of glowing red eyes, until there were none left.

"Good work!" the Professor said, smiling, as they all reached the curved metal underbelly of the *Hive*.

"Frog coming, Max!" Rivet barked. Two wide beams of light sliced through the water and Max glanced back to see Fliktor's dark form swooping towards them.

"Let's get out of here," Max said, diving through the open hatch the cyrates had used. The others followed close behind him.

Inside, Max found himself in a long metal chute which banked steeply upwards. His body thrummed with nerves as he swam along the tube, expecting to meet more cyrates at any moment. The chute became darker and narrower the further they swam, until the only light was the faint glow of Rivet's eyes. Suddenly two points of red appeared ahead. Max's stomach gave a jolt, but then he noticed a metallic sheen around the lights.

"Wait!" he told the others. He swam onwards and found a shiny metal barricade, reflecting the glow of Rivet's eyes. He beckoned Lia and the Professor, then pushed at the metal. His heart filled with relief as it swung open easily, and he led the way through into a brightly lit pool.

Max swam upwards until he broke the surface, then blinked in the harsh white light of a room with a high, domed ceiling, lined with tiles. As the others surfaced, Max scanned the room for any sign of cyrates, but it was empty. He scrambled from the pool and Rivet leapt out behind him, followed by the Professor and Lia.

Lia slipped on her Amphibio mask, then turned to Spike, who looked up at her from the pool. "Stay here," Lia told her swordfish. "You'll be safe from Fliktor, but head to the ocean if any cyrates show up." Spike tipped back his head and let out a trill, then dipped below the surface.

"Riv, can you run a 3D scan of this place?" Max asked his dogbot. "We need to find the source of those mindbugs."

Rivet's eyes flashed as he turned slowly around, scanning the room.

"Done, Max!" Rivet said. Then his eyes turned very bright as they projected a 3D map before him.

"Thanks, Riv!" Max said, examining the spherical map. He recognised the layout from the last time he'd been here – back when he still had hope that there might be some good left in his cousin. Now he almost regretted asking the Coral Giants to spare Siborg's life. *If I hadn't, maybe Aquora wouldn't be in danger now…*

Max rubbed his hands over his face, pushing the thought away, and turned his attention on the map. There was a huge room at the centre with a spiral structure running out from it. Bulkheads formed corridors and chambers along the length of the spiral. Lia pointed to the central room.

"Siborg's lab," she said.

"You're right," Max said. "I'm guessing that's where the mindbugs will be." Max pointed to a glowing green spot not far from the central chamber. "We're here – so if we follow the spiral around, we should arrive at the centre in no time."

There was a circular doorway in the far wall and Max started towards it, beckoning for the others to follow.

He remembered the drab and featureless corridors from their last visit to the *Hive*. Everything was uniformly grey, and lit by harsh white ceiling lights. Max led the way, blaster raised. Rivet stayed close at his side, his nose lifted and twitching.

They followed the curved passage around until they reached the circular doorway that led to the central chamber. But the view through the doorway wasn't at all what Max remembered. Instead of a room full of black, spindly robots, the door now led into a transparent tube, big enough for a person to walk through.

"I think we've found what we were looking for," Max said, shifting his shoulders to get rid of the creeping, tingling feeling.

"And some," Lia breathed. All around the tube, thousands of mindbugs scurried over a curved, rippled structure. It was the colour of flesh, oozing with transparent slime.

Max could hardly believe the scale of what he was looking at.

"A hive within the *Hive*," he said.

CHAPTER SEVEN

SIBORG'S MASTER PLAN

"Utterly fascinating!" the Professor exclaimed, pushing past Max and straight into the mindbug-infested tube.

"Wait!" Max called to the Professor, stepping into the tube behind him.

"But look!" the Professor said. "It's quite extraordinary. Some sort of living material…" He trailed off, pressing his nose against the plastic of the tube. On the other side, mindbugs scurried over the ribs and crests of a fleshy structure. Max shuddered, but thankfully, the bugs didn't seem interested in him. "Extraordinary," the Professor breathed again. Max squeezed past him, and followed the tube onwards with Lia at his side.

"Oh! Now that's just disgusting!" Lia said, wrinkling her nose as a great glob of slime dripped onto the roof of the tube ahead.

Rivet was sniffing at the air, and kept stopping to scratch his metal body.

"Oh, come on!" Max said, waiting for the Professor to tear himself away.

They went around corners and under fleshy pink archways swarming with metal insects. Finally, the tube opened into a lab with a huge holographic globe in the centre.

The Professor immediately strode towards a desk covered in delicate tools and jars of components. But Max was more interested in the holographic display.

"Nemos!" Lia said, as they reached the rotating sphere.

As the globe spun, Max saw all the charted cities of Nemos pass before him, some above the ocean, and some below, but each marked with an ice-blue dot. All except Aquora. As

his home city swung into view, Max saw a glowing red eye hovering over its miniature skyscrapers. Underneath the eye were three glowing words – *Phase One: Complete*.

Max leant forwards and tapped the globe's control panel. Another eye sprang from behind the first, and swept across the globe to hover over Sumara. The words *Phase Two* appeared below it.

Lia gasped. Max tapped the panel again, and two more eyes appeared. One was headed to Verdula, and the other to Gustados. *Phase Three*, said the words.

"His plan of attack," Lia muttered. Max tapped the panel again and again, horror growing in his stomach as more eyes appeared, zipping to every part of the planet.

"Whoa," Lia said. "I knew Siborg was crazy, but he thinks he can take over all of Nemos?"

Max balled his fists. "Well, it's time we

showed him just how wrong he is," he said.

"A noble plan," the Professor called from Siborg's desk. "But if we're going to defeat my son, I'm going to need one of those mindbugs."

Max turned hopefully to Lia. She held up her hands. "Don't look at me!" she said. "Those weird little tech bugs give me the creeps!"

"Riv!" Max said. "Can you fetch a mindbug?" Rivet dropped his nose and curled his tail between his legs. He whined softly.

Max sighed. "Fine!" he said. "I'll do it." He glanced at the revolting, crawling mass through the plastic walls all around them and gritted his teeth. *I've faced fire-throwing Robobeasts. A few tiny Robobugs aren't going to scare me!* He squared his shoulders and stepped towards a zippered door in the plastic that covered the nest.

At the sound of the zip being moved, every one of the bugs stopped still, feelers twitching.

Max cringed as he pulled the zip down the rest of the way and stepped through the flap.

All at once the bugs started moving again, scuttling through the oozing slime. The shivery sound of thousands of tiny movements filled the air. Max reached towards a bug but it darted out of reach. Another took its place and Max made a grab for it, but that one flitted away as well.

"Pssst, Max!" Lia hissed. Max turned to see her holding a long pole with a nozzle on the end through the zippered door. "I think this is for catching them," Lia said. She pushed a trigger on the handle of the pole, and it made a sucking sound.

"Cool!" Max said. He took the vacuum from Lia, and jabbed the nozzle towards a mindbug. The mindbug was sucked into the tube with a pop, where it continued to scurry around, batting its head against the transparent sides.

Max dived back through the doorway and zipped it up behind him, shivering with relief. "Ugh!"

He crossed to the Professor, who had arranged a row of tiny wings and legs on the bench before him. "Ah! Just what I needed," the Professor said, taking the vacuum from Max. "Now, if you don't mind, I'm going to need some peace and quiet."

"Max! Watch out!" Lia cried.

"Cyrates, Max!" Rivet barked.

Max spun, pistol raised, to see cyrates scrambling through the plastic tube that led through the mindbug nest. Lia aimed her blaster at the mouth of the tube as the first cyrate emerged and lifted its gun.

"Careful!" Max cried. "We can't risk damaging the nest and letting the bugs out!"

Lia angled her weapon down towards the cyrate's legs. *Zap!* The cyrate toppled, its legs blasted in half.

"Nice shot!" Max said, finishing the evil robot off with a shot to the head.

The next cyrate was already emerging from the tunnel, and Max and Lia fired again.

Zap! The cyrate toppled and its head exploded. Cyrate after cyrate poured towards them, and Max and Lia fired over and over, until Max was sweating and his arm was

aching from the strain. Finally, when he was beginning to worry they couldn't possibly keep up the pace, the stream of cyrates stopped and Max found himself standing before a mound of twitching metal bodies.

Lia blinked at the pile of robots, then turned to Max with a grin. "I think I'm getting the hang of this!" she said. Max gave her a high five, and turned toward the Professor.

"How are you doing?" he asked.

"Well, I can hardly call that peace and quiet," the Professor said, "but not too badly. These bugs are even more fascinating than I thought. Look here." The Professor pointed towards a bulge on the underbelly of the bug he was holding. "This is a renewable power supply. It's very clever because –"

"But have you worked out how to deactivate it?" Max cut in.

"Oh yes, I managed that quite quickly. But the better I understand these things, the more help I can be."

"How about the quicker we get out of here, the less likely we are to be blasted to smithereens?" Lia said.

The Professor stood up slowly, with a sigh. "I suppose you're right. After all, I'm unlikely to get my pardon if you get yourselves killed."

"Oh, don't go yet," a familiar, emotionless voice suddenly said through speakers in the ceiling. *Siborg!* Max thought with a jolt of fear. *He must have a hidden camera!*

"You have exceeded my expectations once again," Siborg went on, "which means I can have even more fun with you! Let's see how you deal with this, cousin."

A grating sound echoed up from the bowels of the ship. The metal deck beneath Max's feet began to judder.

"That doesn't sound good," Lia said, glancing around the quivering room. Rivet dropped to his belly by Max's feet and Max lifted his blaster, ready for an attack. Suddenly the trembling stopped. But another sound filled the air. The sound of rushing water.

The roaring and rushing got louder and louder until it seemed to be all around them.

"Brace yourselves!" Max cried. "It sounds like a tidal wave's coming our way!"

CHAPTER EIGHT

ENEMIES EVERYWHERE

A jet of water shot from the plastic tube, knocking Lia off her feet. *Siborg's flooding his own ship!* Max realised. He staggered and fell as water swirled around him, churning and foaming, tugging him under. He tried to swim against the flow, but it was no use.

Max caught a glimpse of Lia struggling with her Amphibio mask as she shot away, snatched up by the current. The mindbugs

scurried around her, protected by their
plastic home. The Professor whooshed
after Lia, arms flailing and eyes wide with
surprise. Max's stomach flipped as a current
caught hold of him, and tugged him along
too. The mindbug hive flashed by in a blur as
he whizzed along the plastic tube, then out
into the grey corridors of the ship.

Ceiling lights swept past as Max sped around looping corridors, swooping and diving headfirst, until finally he burst through a hatch and into the calm silence of the open ocean.

He shook his head to clear his senses. He could see the Professor and Lia nearby, and Rivet powering towards him. Spikc burst from another hatch on the side of the ship, tumbling over and over in a swirl of bubbles, until he came to a stop beside Lia.

"Well, that was fun," Lia said, letting Spike nuzzle her cheek.

Max nodded, puzzled. "I don't know why Siborg thought flooding the ship would be an issue for us. He knows we can breathe underwater."

"I rather suspect that he isn't finished with us yet," the Professor said. He pointed into the ocean, just as two beams of white light flashed towards them, and came to rest on Lia.

Max's heart leapt as Fliktor's silvery tongue snaked towards her. Spike let out a trill of alarm.

"Watch out!" Max cried, diving towards his friend. But Fliktor's tongue lashed around her waist and tugged her away.

"Ahhhh!" Lia cried.

Max swam as fast as he could, trying to catch hold of Lia's outstretched hands, but she was snatched away from him into the deep, dark water ahead. Spike darted after her, letting out a frenzy of warning clicks.

Max stared at the space where Lia had been, horrified, the picture of her frightened eyes etched into his mind. Then he shook his head and gritted his teeth. *I have to save her!*

He kicked his legs and powered towards the lights of Fliktor's eyes, just as the ocean around him lit up with red energy bolts. Rivet let out a growl, and Max glanced back to see his dogbot's jaws wrapped around the arm of a cyrate. The Professor was swinging his hyperblade, hacking at another robot, while more streamed from the flooded *Hive* into the sea. An energy bolt zapped past Max's cheek, so close he felt the heat of it.

He glanced again at Fliktor and could see

Lia silhouetted against the light from the robot's eyes, her body jerking up and down as Fliktor's tongue whipped her about. The sight of her fragile body so close to the Robobeast's colossal rocket launchers made Max's blood run cold. Spike was thrusting and jabbing at the coil that held Lia, but Fliktor was too fast for him, and kept whipping his tongue out of reach. Max pulled his aquafly's remote control from his pocket and jabbed a button, hoping his craft hadn't been too damaged by Fliktor to respond. He felt a rush of relief as it surged towards him from out of the depths. Then he tapped in a command, programming his craft to lock onto the cyrates. The aquafly sped past him, and Max glanced back to see it open fire on a group of cyrates that were zooming past the Professor and Rivet.

He swallowed hard and turned back to Lia.

Spike was still swooping through the water, clicking and screeching. Lia was hanging limply as the robot jerked her about.

Max kicked towards the Robobeast, his blaster raised. But with Spike swimming so close to the creature's jaws, he couldn't get a clear shot.

"Spike!" Max cried, hoping the swordfish would understand what he meant. "Go and help Rivet! I'll save Lia!" Spike darted away, and Max tried to take aim again, but he couldn't risk harming Lia. Her hair was hanging over her face, and he couldn't tell if she was still conscious. He felt sick with worry and fear. *How can I help her?* Then he had a thought. *Fliktor's under Siborg's control. If Siborg wanted to kill Lia, Fliktor could have opened fire by now.* Then Max realised. *It's me Siborg hates more than anyone else in Nemos. Lia's just bait.*

Max let his blaster fall from his hand and swam into the beam of the robot's eyes.

"Hey! Fliktor!" Max said, squinting against the light. "Let Lia go. It's not her you're after, it's me." Max held up his hands, showing the giant frog he was unarmed. The robot's eyes seemed to fade for a moment. Then they flicked from harsh white to fiery red. Fliktor's tongue slowly uncoiled and Lia swam free. Max felt a rush of relief to see she was unharmed, then turned back to the robotic beast. Fliktor's huge red eyes surged towards him, and its mouth opened, revealing rows of spiked torpedoes.

"Max, no!" Lia shouted.

Max felt the current swirl around him. Fliktor's metal tongue lashed about his chest, jerking his whole body so hard he saw stars. Max's stomach was left behind as he was snatched through the water and into the

depths of Fliktor's mouth.

Then the robot's jaws snapped shut,
plunging him into darkness.

CHAPTER NINE

JUST THE BEGINNING

Max gasped in agony at the terrible crushing pain around his chest where Fliktor's tongue held him tight. He tried to suck water over his gills and realised with building panic that he couldn't breathe. His pulse thudded and his lungs burned as he thrashed his arms and legs in the darkness. But the more he moved, the dizzier he became. Soon he could see red spots forming at the sides of his vision. He shook his head, forcing himself to stay calm. *I can't escape Fliktor's tongue, so I'll have to disable it.*

Max glanced around. There was a faint, flashing light coming from above his head — a row of blinking LEDs on the roof of the robot's mouth. *The control box!*

Max reached a hand upwards towards the row of lights. The pain in his chest was tremendous as he stretched, and he felt sickness building inside him. He lowered his arm, reeling with pain and nausea. But he had to try again.

He reached up, ignoring how much it hurt. *I've battled sharks and crocodiles!* Max told himself. *There is no way I'm getting eaten by a frog!* Max's fingers grabbed the cover of the control box and pulled it open. Inside there was a mass of shiny glass tubes and wires.

He took hold of a handful of components and tugged, hoping they were the right ones.

If he destroyed the wrong part, the tongue might squeeze even harder. The wires came away in his fingers and the lights went out.

Max waited in the darkness, his whole body screaming with pain. Then, suddenly, the hideous, bone-crushing force around his chest relaxed. He drew a huge gulp of water over his gills and felt a wave of relief as his head started to clear.

He dived forwards, reaching blindly in the darkness for Fliktor's closed lips. His hands hit metal, and he found a narrow groove, then tugged, trying to prise the mouth open. It wouldn't budge. Max tried again, but the metal was held tightly shut by the robot's hydraulic jaws. *No!*

Max thought of the handful of wires he'd removed with a stab of realisation. He'd destroyed the Robobeast, but now he was stuck inside it! And there was no way he could repair the control box in darkness. Max felt anxiety swelling inside him. Without power, Fliktor would be drifting downwards towards the ocean bed. Max couldn't help thinking of all the sailors and explorers who had ended their days by sinking silently into the depths. He pushed again at Fliktor's jaws, wedging his feet against the floor of the robot's mouth and his hands against the roof. But it was useless.

"Lia!" Max shouted. But his voice echoed back to him, reverberating around and around in Fliktor's metal head.

Max swallowed, forcing his growing panic aside so he could think. Then suddenly he saw a tiny chink of light. Fliktor's jaws had opened a crack, and the tip of Spike's sword was poking through.

"Spike!" Max cried. Lia's webbed fingers appeared at the gap. Max darted forwards and braced himself against Fliktor's jaws, adding his strength to theirs. Slowly but surely, the metal mouth opened. Max's muscles were burning and he was shaking with the effort, but he could see his friends outside. As soon as the gap was wide enough, Max darted out into the open ocean, sucking cool, clean water over his gills.

Rivet licked his face and Spike clicked happily as Fliktor's body sank into the depths below. Lia's eyes shone with relief as she looked Max over.

"Thank goodness you're all in one piece," she said. "I was seriously worried about what I would find when we got that evil robot's mouth open."

"Speaking of evil," Max said, "where did the Professor go?" Lia opened her mouth to answer, but her words were drowned out by the throb of mighty engines powering up. The sound was coming from the *Hive*.

Max turned to see the giant ship gliding away from them through the rocky water.

"The Professor's stealing the *Hive*!" he cried. "He must have wanted the mindbug technology all along." But as Max watched, he saw that the *Hive* wasn't headed for open water. Instead, it was sailing towards the craggy side of the underwater mountain.

"It's going to crash!" Lia said.

"But we need the Professor to destroy the mindbugs," Max said, feeling cold all over.

Max and Lia stared, open-mouthed, as the *Hive* ploughed into the side of the mountain. A groaning crunch echoed through the ocean as the side of the ship bucked and folded in

on itself. The shriek of tearing metal and splintering rock went on and on and the seabed trembled.

BOOM! The ship suddenly erupted into a great mushroom of flame. Max was thrown backwards, tumbling over in the churning sea. Silt and bits of broken metal flew past as the water tugged at his body. Then everything went suddenly still. The shockwave had passed. Max saw Rivet and Lia on Spike right themselves and start swimming towards him.

He was glad to see them safe, but he couldn't shake the feeling of horror that had gripped hold of him when the *Hive* had crashed. *The Professor was our only hope of defeating the mindbugs*, he thought. *The only hope of saving Dad…*

"Well, that worked even better than I expected," a familiar voice said from nearby. Max turned to see the Professor paddling towards him, his face smeared with soot. "There were lots of vicious cyrates in there," the Professor said. "It got a bit sticky towards the end, but I took care of them. And then I found this." The Professor held up a remote control, not too different to Max's fetchpad.

"You destroyed the *Hive*?" Max said.

"Of course," replied the Professor. "We didn't want those nasty bugs crawling all over the place, did we? And anyway, we got what we came for." He held up a jar with a shiny blue beetle inside, lying on its back.

"Then you know how to shut the bugs down?" Lia asked.

The Professor nodded. "It's fairly easy at close range," he said. "Destroying them from a safe distance is going to be a bit more of a challenge. But I have an idea of how we can do it. In one of my labs, I have an experimental raygun. If I can modify it,

we should be able to destroy the bugs by
firing it at their host. But we have very little
time, if we want to avoid accidentally killing
everyone in Aquora."

"What do you mean?" Max said.

"Well," the Professor said, "it seems that if
a mindbug is attached for too long, the host

becomes dependent on it to stay alive. Past that point, deactivating them would be fatal."

Max felt sick at the thought of his father and all of his neighbours becoming possessed by the mindbugs for good.

"How long do we have?" he asked.

"I'm not precisely sure," the Professor said, "but let's just say we don't have time to float around here chatting."

Max took a deep breath, and nodded. "Let's go, then!" he said. He pulled his fetchpad from his pocket, and summoned the aquafly. He still wasn't sure about working with the Professor, and he definitely didn't trust the man, but he wasn't about to let Aquora turn into a city of cyber zombies either.

The Sea Quest was on. And this time both his parents' lives depended on him.

Don't miss Max's next Sea Quest adventure,
when he faces

TENGAL
THE SAVAGE SHARK

Look out for all the books in
Sea Quest Series 7:

THE LOST STARSHIP

VELOTH THE VAMPIRE SQUID
GLENDOR THE STEALTHY SHADOW
MIRROC THE GOBLIN SHARK
BLISTRA THE SEA DRAGON

OUT IN MARCH 2016!

Don't miss the
BRAND NEW
Special Bumper Edition:
JANDOR
THE ARCTIC LIZARD

OUT IN NOVEMBER 2015

WIN AN EXCLUSIVE GOODY BAG

In every Sea Quest book the Sea Quest logo is hidden in one of the pictures. Find the logos in books 21-24, make a note of which pages they appear on and go online to enter the competition at

www.seaquestbooks.co.uk

Each month we will put all of the correct entries into a draw and select one winner to receive a special Sea Quest goody bag.

You can also send your entry on a postcard to:

Sea Quest Competition, Orchard Books, Carmelite House, 50 Victoria Embankment, London, EC4Y 0DZ

Don't forget to include your name and address!

GOOD LUCK

Closing Date: Dec 30th 2015

IF YOU LIKE SEA QUEST, YOU'LL LOVE BEAST QUEST!

Series 1: COLLECT THEM ALL!

An evil wizard has enchanted the magical beasts of Avantia. Only a true hero can free the beasts and save the land. Is Tom the hero Avantia has been waiting for?

FERNO
THE FIRE DRAGON
978 1 84616 483 5

SEPRON
THE SEA SERPENT
978 1 84616 482 8

ARCTA
THE MOUNTAIN GIANT
978 1 84616 484 2

TAGUS
THE HORSE MAN
978 1 84616 486 6

NANOOK
THE SNOW MONSTER
978 1 84616 485 9

EPOS
THE FLAME BIRD
978 1 84616 487 3